MY ADVENTURES WITH

SPIDER-MAN

This book was especially written for
Channing Olinger
with love from
GAM GAM & Papa Brad

By Kate Andresen
Illustrated by The Artifact Group
ISBN 978-1-875676-27-9

PETER PARKER

Peter Parker was once a regular teenager. When he was bitten by a radioactive spider, he was empowered with the arachnid's proportional strength and agility.

SPIDER-MAN

Peter Parker became a crime-fighting super-hero, known as Spider-Man.

J. JONAH JAMESON

Peter worked at the Daily Bugle newspaper as a freelance photographer. His job was to provide pictures of himself as Spider-Man to J. Jonah Jameson, the editor.

DOCTOR OCTOPUS

Doctor Octavius was a brilliant scientist working on a new invention until a laboratory accident fused a set of mechanical arms to his body and turned him into the dreaded super-villain, Doctor Octopus.

Channing Olinger was at home in Huntington, waiting for the mail to arrive. To his delight, there was a letter addressed to him from the Daily Bugle newspaper in New York.

He ripped open the envelope and read the letter.

"Wow!" exclaimed Channing. "I've won a trip to New York! And Brooklynn and Donovan can come, too."

DAILY BUGLE

Congratulations Channing! You are the winner of the Daily Bugle Amateur Photographic competition. Your prize is to spend a week in our office where we will help you to develop your photographic skills. Enclosed are return air tickets to New York for you and three friends. Look forward to seeing you!

J. Jonah Jameson

Editor

At the Daily Bugle offices, the editor, J. Jonah Jameson, announced to his staff,

"Tomorrow, the winner of the Amateur Photographic competition will be joining us for a week."

"Parker, I want you to accompany the kid and your assignment is to track down Spider-Man and finally reveal his identity."

Channing arrived at the Daily Bugle offices where he was met by Mr Jameson and Peter Parker.

"Welcome, Channing! I have a special assignment for you. Spider-Man has been popping up all over town lately and I'd like you and Peter Parker here to find him! Whilst you're here with us, I'll arrange for Brooklynn and Donovan to take in the sights of our great city."

Channing had heard about Spider-Man's heroic deeds and was very excited!

"Grab your camera, Channing!" called Peter Parker. "Let's go and find Spider-Man!"

Of course, Peter Parker couldn't reveal his secret identity, but he did try to explain that Spider-Man always used his super powers for good.

"Many villains have tried to destroy the city and harm the people of New York, but Spider-Man is always there to help out. He has become a super-hero and people want to know who he is."

Walking down 5th Avenue, Peter pointed out the Empire State Building.

Channing looked up in awe at the building that rose majestically above the city skyline.

Suddenly, Channing heard people screaming and shouting, "Stop! Stop!"

Then … CRASH, he was knocked to the pavement. He looked up and saw a man running away.

But this was no ordinary man. He had four huge
metal arms sticking out of his back, and each one was
clutching bags full of money!

"It's Doc Ock!" exclaimed Peter. "He's robbed a
bank!"

As Channing scrambled to his feet, he saw Doctor Octopus escaping down the street. Suddenly, Spider-Man appeared and chased after Doctor Octopus.

"Peter, there's Spider-Man!" called Channing. But Peter was nowhere to be seen.

Remembering Mr Jameson's instructions, Channing ran after them. He hoped Peter would follow!

As Doctor Octopus ran away, his metal arms waved about frantically, knocking over pedestrians and anything else that got in his way.

Spider-Man ducked and weaved as he tried desperately to catch the villain.

Doctor Octopus and Spider-Man left behind them a trail of upturned garbage bins, broken tree branches and frightened pedestrians.

Channing sped after them, taking as many photographs as he could of the villain and the super-hero.

As Spider-Man drew closer to Doctor Octopus, he shot a web at him but he was able to brush it aside. Doctor Octopus was angry! He grabbed a passing car and hurled it at Spider-Man.

It caught Spider-Man by surprise, and he collapsed on the pavement, stunned.

When Channing caught up to Spider-Man, he saw that he was hurt and he lay still on the pavement.

"Oh no, Doc Ock will get away. What can I do?" exclaimed Channing.

Doctor Octopus yelled, "That'll teach you to mess with me, Spider-Man!" and he ran off, still clutching the bags of money.

Channing knelt down beside Spider-Man. He gently lifted his head and whispered to him, "Focus on your powers and your strength will return."

Soon, with Channing's help, Spider-Man got to his feet and they ran after Doctor Octopus.

They followed Doctor Octopus round a corner.
There was a line of police cars blocking the street.
Policemen were crouching behind their cars, aiming
their weapons at Doctor Octopus.

"Stop! Drop the money!" yelled a policeman.

"Make me!" growled Doctor Octopus as he leaped over the cars, grabbed a policeman in each arm and hurled them high into the air.

People were screaming and running for cover as Doctor Octopus continued his rampage.

In the chaos, Channing saw Brooklynn and Donovan running towards them.

"Quick everyone! Over here!" called Channing. He pulled them into a doorway.

"You'll be safe here for now but make your way to the Daily Bugle offices and I'll see you there. Spider-Man will save us!" he said as he ran off in pursuit.

Spider-Man was following every move Doctor Octopus made, scaling buildings and swinging between the skyscrapers. He was close, but just not close enough to capture Doc Ock!

Channing watched as Doctor Octopus scrambled down the side of the building above him and landed with a loud THUMP in front of him.

"So you're the one that's been helping Spider-Man are you?" Doc Ock asked angrily. "A friend of Spider-Man's is no friend of mine!"

Doc Ock grabbed hold of Channing ran across the street and clambered up the side of a tall, glass skyscraper.

"Help, help!" Channing screamed.

But Spider-Man had anticipated Doc Ock's next move and he was waiting at the top of the building. When Doc Ock reached the top, Spider-Man shot webs at him and pinned down his arms.

Doc Ock dropped Channing on the window ledge as he struggled to free himself.

Channing was very frightened and he gripped the ledge tightly. All he could do was watch as Spider-Man and Doc Ock fought desperately.

Fighting someone with eight limbs was not easy!
Doc Ock grabbed Spider-Man and smashed him
through the side of the building. Doc Ock crashed
through the window after him.

Channing carefully crawled along the window ledge and climbed in through the broken window. Inside, terrified office workers scrambled out of the way. Doc Ock's long arms kicked and punched anything that moved.

Channing hid behind an upturned desk.

"You'll never get away with this!" cried Spider-Man as he shot a web at a nearby desk and hurled it at Doc Ock.

"You're no match for me!" yelled Doc Ock.

Doc Ock caught the desk and swung it above his head. As Doc Ock was about to hurl the desk back at Spider-Man, Channing rushed out from where he was hiding and dived at Doc Ock's legs.

As Doctor Octopus stumbled and fell, Spider-Man
shot webs at him, enclosing him in a tight web.

"Well done, Channing!" exclaimed Spider-Man.

"We did it!" replied Channing. Channing took out his camera that he had been hiding inside his shirt and took a photograph of Spider-Man standing next to the defeated Doctor Octopus.

Soon the police arrived and arrested Doctor Octopus.

"You'll be locked up for a long time!" said Spider-Man as Doctor Octopus was being taken away.

"Don't bet on it!" replied Doc Ock.

The next day, New York was buzzing with the news and the front page of the Daily Bugle read:

DAILY BUGLE

SPIDER-MAN AND CHANNING OLINGER SAVE THE DAY!

Spider-Man, with the help of Channing Olinger of Huntington, has captured the super-villain, Doctor Octopus. A reception in Channing's honor will be held at the Town Hall this afternoon so that the people of New York can personally thank the young hero.

In front of thousands of people, the mayor presented Channing with a gold medal that was engraved with: New York honors Channing Olinger, October 14, 2014.

Brooklynn and Donovan looked on with pride! It was an extra special day, as October 14th was Channing's birthday.

Mr Jameson and Peter Parker were also at the reception.

"Well, we got some great pictures of Spider-Man but we still don't know who he is!" Mr Jameson said to Peter Parker.

Peter smiled. His secret was safe.

This personalized Marvel Spider-Man book was especially created for
Channing Olinger of 722 N GROVER ST, Huntington, with love from GAM GAM
& Papa Brad.

If Channing loved starring in this personalized My Adventure Book then there
are many more exciting stories in our collection.

Simply visit us at www.identitydirect.com to create
Channing's next adventure!

Alternatively, you can contact us by phone on 224 265 6363.

Lots of exciting titles to collect!

0958 002685 0002 01 DM 0135

Order Ref #6687648